Jill Gets Fit

CHARACTERS

Jill's Brain

Jill's Heart

Jill's Lungs

Jill's Eyes

Jill's Stomach

Jill's Legs and Hands

SETTING

Jill's house

Brain: Quiet, please! Since I am the Brain, I call this meeting of Jill's body to order!

Heart: Why are we meeting? What's the problem?

Brain: Jill's in trouble. She's not taking care of herself.

Lungs: What kind of trouble?

Brain: She's tired all the time. She has no energy. Does anybody know what she does all day?

Eyes: I'm her Eyes, and I see what she does—nothing but watch TV!

Stomach: Right! And she eats too much candy and drinks too much soda. It hurts me to even think about it.

Brain: Stomach, we have to help Jill feel better. She needs to eat better and exercise so she'll have energy.

Lungs: Exercise? What's that?

Brain: It's doing such things as jumping, running, and playing ball. Swimming and bike riding are good exercise, too.

Lungs: Oh, I love exercise!

Heart: We'd all feel better if Jill got exercise. I pump the blood through Jill's body. But all she does is sit around.

Legs: We have nothing to do. We need to run around if we're going to be strong.

Heart: This isn't going to be easy.

Brain: Eyes, do you have any ideas?

Eyes: We're tired of watching TV. We need light. Let's get her outside.

Brain: How about you, Legs?

Legs: We agree with Eyes. She should go outside and play with her friends.

Heart: I think she should join a team at school.

Brain: Lungs, what do you think?

Lungs: I agree with Heart. She could join a team at school, or she could just play with her friends.

Stomach: Maybe you guys are bored, but I'm not. I'm working all the time.

Heart: Poor Stomach! All that awful food!

Eyes: Jill needs to eat more healthful food. We read that in a book.

Brain: That's an idea! I'll get Jill to reread that book. Legs, get moving. Hands, pick up the book.

Legs and **Hands**: Got it!

Eyes: Hey, look! She's reading it.

Brain: She's reading the part about eating good food. Now she's reading the part about exercise.

Eyes: Oh, no! She's closing the book!

Legs: But she's getting up!

Heart: She turned off the TV!

Lungs: She's going out to play!

Stomach: Quick! Let's get a healthful snack for Jill. Some fresh fruit...a glass of milk...

Eyes: Good. She's not even looking at the candy and soda.

Stomach: Oh, that feels much better!

Legs: She's going outside. She's starting to run.

Heart: Oooh! This is great. Good food is on the way, and I'm pumping blood rich in oxygen.

Brain: Is everyone happy now?

Eyes: Wow! Look at the sky and the trees! It's fun being out here.

Lungs: Smell the fresh air! Breathe in. Breathe out.

Heart: Thanks for the air, Lungs. Now I can pump Jill's blood faster. What fun! Let's go, Legs!

Stomach: She's found some friends. They're playing soccer. She's joining them.

Legs: We're running at last! Look at us go!

Lungs: Jill is having fun, too.

Eyes: Look at her smile!

Heart: We're a great team when we work together.

Brain: OK, guys. We'll meet again tomorrow—same time, same place. Let's ride our bikes!

All: We'll be there!

The End